THE MUSE OF WYNTER

A Winter's Fairy Tale

& A PREVIEW CHAPTER FROM

CALL OF THE STORM SORCERER

The Serpntine Throne Book 1

by SUSAN STRADIOTTO

COPYRIGHT NOTICE

THE MUSE OF WYNTER

A Winter's Fairy Tale

SUSAN STRADIOTTO

THE HIGH PRIESTESS OF Muses stood on the Cliffs of Change. Volumptuous ceremonial robes woven of winter's silver and summer's gold billowed behind where she stood. Her mane, the bluest black, danced as a flag animated by Wind. Her bare feet caressed the cool stone as the Wind swept the storm clouds into a pile above. Nestled beneath the cliffs in River's Vale laid Ripplemere, a village divided by a river of the same name. The forefathers had named the village after the flowing seas they'd traveled before colonizing the valley. A scream rolled uphill to where High Priestess kept her vigil, a message delivered crisply by Wind. In his wail, the awaited signal emerged. Waters had broken. The High Priestess turned from the cliffs, hoping Nellwyn was ready.

$\mathbf{A}$ ROOM IN CHAOS; NOT a soul took notice of the visitor who sat on the windowsill, cleaning her wings. The visitor tried not to watch until her moment arrived. Giants in white tended to the bedded mother giant whose mane hung lank around her reddened face. The mother giant's patterned breathing kept time as a metronome to music. Her melody, howling moans grew into screams and faded into small, mewling whines. With each crescendo, she hunched tighter around the bulge of her midsection. On lingering whimpers, the visitor looked up to see if it was done. Hours passed as the visitor waited amidst the bustle and hum of voices punctuated by a mother's agony. The visitor remained vigilant. This was not a time to rest. Important work awaited.

At long last, when the baby giant slipped from the mother, the small visitor's wings perked. This was the signal she awaited. Lifting her wings, she fluttered to the shoulder of the mother. There she waited . . . unseen . . . unheard. She clasped hands to her chest, watching, eager to glimpse. Long seasons of training had prepared her. And now her work began.

The giants in white shrieked in surprise. Whispers echoed loud in the visitor's sensitive ears—much louder than they sounded to the other giants, but so many that the visitor could not discern a single thought. Never seen anything like . . . That mane . . . Check her eyes . . . Not red . . . Get the midwife. One of the white-clothed giants swaddled the babe. A rotund giant scurried—as fast as a portly giant can—to the door.

"Midwife!" she bawled down the hall.

The mother giant struggled against her own heavy limbs to get to the child, already feeling the acute loss of separation. The father giant was not yet so bonded. That would only come when he looked into the babe's eyes. Then she would become real. In that moment, he cared only for this exhausted woman and hugged her down to encourage rest. He'd felt helpless through her ordeal. But now, he assured her that their baby would be fine. That she was in the best of hands. That he was there to protect them both.

The white giants took the swaddle and left, evoking new screams from the mother. These screams were different, ones that keened with anger and loss. The room fell silent, save for the mother's sobs. The air grew heavier with every moment that passed. There was no one to tend to the mother giant except the father, and his expertise laid only in working metal. Steadfast at the mother's shoulder, the visitor watched the woman's reddened face grow pale. Dark strands plastered themselves to her cheeks. Father giant brushed the strands back, kissing her hands, cheeks, forehead, and making soft noises to shush her pain.

One of the white-clad giants, hair wrapped in cloth, returned, smiling as she brought in the bundle. She placed the bundle in the mother giant's arms, and said, "You have a happy, healthy baby girl with quite the unusual mane."

The mother's features turned from drawn and wrinkled to smooth. She laid back on the bed. Her eyes opened, and her mouth formed an O as she locked eyes with her child.

From the mother's shoulder, gazing at the babe, the visitor whispered, "Wynter."

The three in the room couldn't hear. But the baby giggled, and the mother giant shivered. The father smiled at his happy family. Despite the joy, the visitor, on her shoulder-seat, cried tiny streams of silver. For she knew the white-clad giants wouldn't help. They were not able. This was the mother giant's destiny, but that didn't make it a happy fate.

Tiny coal-black eyes looked wide at her mother, staring from under a snow-white thicket. It was a baby's mane—fine as silk, but it was thicker than the giants could imagine on a newborn child. The mother giant kissed the white silk and raised weak eyes, full of love to the child's father.

A shout—urgent pleas for help—ripped through the room. The white-robed giant noted the red swimming across the bed linens between the mother giant's legs. She ran from the room, down the hall, to bring the doctor. But her alarm arose too late.

In her threadbare voice, the mother giant said, "Darling, I know we discussed naming her Nicole." She paused again to love her daughter with her eyes, to touch her cheek to the bundle's tiny pink cheek, to lay a kiss on the child's brow. "But looking at her now, I think we should name her Wynter."

Pools flooded into Darling's eyes. He looked between his wife and his new daughter. In that instant, he knew that only two of them would leave the room alive. He shook away the image of his lovely wife sailing across the great sea. Then he granted the mother of his child her last wish. "Wynter, it is.' As her arms went limp, Darling caught Wynter and hugged her close. A tear leaking from the pool, down his face, and dampening a wisp of Wynter's snow-white mane.

WYNTER WAS AN EASY child who mended and enlarged her father's heart. In the earliest of days, when he held his daughter, he knew not if he cried from a father's love or a husband's heartbreak. From the start, Wynter afforded Darling six hours of sleep every night. When she awoke in her cradle, she giggled at the antics of the visitor who had come home from the hospital on Darling's shoulder.

The only displeasure Wynter ever expressed was when Darling returned to work. He had no one to care for the child, but he had an area in the smithy where she could coo all day in the cradle. When the forges were lit, and the air warmed to a sweat, her little cries troubled Darling and his other smith, Ben. The visitor watched as the burly giants took turns holding and walking Wynter outside the forge while the other worked. On the second day, the giant in Darling's employ brought his wife and wee giants to the forge.

The giant wife admonished Darling. "Abner, you mustn't expose the wee girl to the fires!" She scooped Wynter in her arms and rushed from the smithy with wee giants on her skirts. As she scurried through the exit, she told Abner to come home with Ben for evening meal, and once his belly was stretched, he could take his dear Wynter home for the eve.

The visitor fluttered from the smithy with the giant wife so not to lose her charge. This woman's rebuke was the first time she had heard Wynter's father's name. The visitor decided she preferred Darling, the name spoken with ardor by the mother of Wynter upon her deathbed.

And so Time, a knitting crone, wove the days, stitched the weeks, and slipped the threads into months. Wynter and the visitor spent their days cooing with the wee giants and their nights tucked into the home hut with Darling.

It was an unusually warm day that threaded into evening. Wynter was abnormally fussy that day. At dinner with Darling, Ben, Ben's wife, and Ben's wee ones, Wynter cried. On her cries, Wind answered with a whistle through the hut, and the night cooled. When the evening chilled to her satisfaction, Wynter became happy once more. As the extended family sipped the after-dinner cordial, Wynter spoke for the first time.

Darling spilled his drink as he jumped at the musical sound. He rushed over to Wynter, words swirling together. "Did you hear that? —Was that her first word? —What did she say?" His voice slowed and softened when he finally asked, "Can you say it again, Wynter?"

"Nellwyn," she said with a tinkling laugh and pointed to Darling's shoulder. A single, glistening, love-filled drop landed on Darling's shirt. The visitor Nellwyn wept.

AS TIME SPUN THAT first year into two, then three, Wynter grew as any normal child grows. Her white mane lengthened and thickened, but the color never changed. Her sparkling-winged friend, Nellwyn, was forever by her side—doing her sworn duty, protecting, inspiring. Although her duty had sweetened to love, and to leave the child became a thought as painful as ripping the wings from her own back.

Wynter awoke with swollen eyes on the morning after her first truly beastly choler. The air had crispened. When she peered outside her turf-roofed hut, the trees had changed. No longer did they carry their verdant leaves. The green had turned golden, auburn, and bitter-sweet orange. And though it seemed her tantrum erased the greenery and brought the colder air, Wynter still had the warmest of hearts. She loved the feel of the sun on her face as she picked fall dandelions and scattered their seeds on Wind's voice. Then she played a repeated game with her friend Nellwyn, chasing and catching the floating white fuzz. Nellwyn shared the child's joy in a game that was all their own. Wynter loved the feel of the earth on her feet and adamantly refused to be shod. Every day, she would pad to the Ripplemere that ran by her hut and relish the cool tide washing over her toes.

The name of Ben's wife, Wynter's daytime caretaker, was forever a mystery. He called her Woman. But when he did, it brought a shy sparkle to her eyes and color to her cheeks. As Time knitted away the years, Woman's wee giants, Darcy and Digby, grew to pint-sized giants along with Wynter. Woman split the days between her hut and Wynter's. Oft it was, when forges were silent, that Ben, Woman, Darcy, Digby, Darling, and Wynter would gather in Darling's hut. On a particularly cool morn, Wynter watched as Nellwyn lit on Woman's shoulder. With an unheard whisper, Nellwyn set an idea upon Woman.

When Woman sat Darling down at the kitchen table of his own hut for a long talk, she shooed Wynter and her child giants outside. But Wynter and Nellwyn snuck to the rear and crouched beneath window. To Darling, Woman said that it was time for Wynter to see the village maestro. Silence stretched and shattered when the chair careened against the stone floor. Darling's boot heels marked his nearing the window. As he gazed down the knoll, he spoke his fatherly fears to Woman—of cost, of time beyond means. But Woman urged him on, and with the dawn, the doting father giant took Wynter to the music man's shop down the river.

Nellwyn sat on the wizened man's shoulder and whispered sweet nothings. Set deep within a small pink face framed by a wild white mane and significant beard, the maestro's black eyes twinkled, and he clasped his hands, pulling them to his chin. Then, with a finger to the red tip of his nose, he said, "I have just the thing for this lovely white-maned girl."

With a hop in his step that belied his age, he skipped off to the back room. Some shuffling and a sequence of thuds later, he returned with a case taller by half than Wynter herself. He grinned and scurried away again, only to return with a long and slender box. With both laid on the counter before him, he guided Wynter to a chair. Nellwyn bounced and fluttered down on the counter, waiting for Maestro to open the case. Finally, with wide eyes, he lifted the case lid. The worn wood hinged to lie flat, and from the case emerged a crystal violoncello. Slowly, and every so gently, Maestro placed it on the counter. Light gathered in the facets and sprayed rainbows on the walls of the hut.

Maestro crossed the room to where Wynter sat and raised her chair with eyes rounded. Nellwyn's wings buzzed as she floated to the teacher giant's shoulder. There she rode as he retrieved the instrument and placed it reverently between Wynter's knees.

"Hold it just there, love." Maestro guided her hands, then turned to the slender, unopened box. Opening one end, he withdrew a long bow, white ivory handled and hairs from a white stallion threaded tight. Maestro placed the handle of the bow in Wynter's hand and guided her small hand to draw the hairs across the strings. The tenor note rolled through the room and out the window. In a whistling rush, Wind replied with a cold rush, lifting the manes of all in the room.

Maestro's smile split his beard.

Nellwyn applauded.

TIME'S TAPESTRY GREW—AS IS only right for her work. She fed and watered Wynter and her near-sibling giants, Darcy and Digby, so that their bodies ripened. As boys, naturally Time shared more nourishment for Darcy and Digby than she did for Wynter, but that was well. Darcy and Digby cared much for the small sister that Woman couldn't provide, and their size protected their little white-maned Wynter.

With her accursed knife, Age carved streambeds at the corner of Darling's, Ben's, and Woman's eyes. She cut canyons, framing their smiles. Darling never remarried, but the six of them lived closely—as family. Companionship was never amiss in Darling's mind. He had his Wynter. But, at times, Darling spent long evening hours staring into the hearth, bringing his giant wife back to life if only in his mind's eye. In those evenings, even though Wynter despised the flame, she sat by her father's side and held his hand. At his other side, nestled inside Darling's collar, unfelt, and unheard, Nellwyn nuzzled his neck and whispered sweet soothing nothings.

Having the twin giants, and with Ben and Darling, Wynter never wanted for absent family. And having Woman, she never longed for an absent mother giant. And she had Nellwyn. In those intimate family moments—Woman's look that corrected wrongs; Darling's proud regard as Wynter caught seeds carried by Wind; Ben's jovial banter with Darling; the men giants and the boy giants playing rough in the grassy knoll; Darcy or Digby sweeping Wynter into their arms—Nellwyn's tiny heart swelled such that her tiny body could not contain the joy. She dripped sparkling tears onto those she now claimed as her own giant family. They were blessed.

Wynter, Darcy, and Digby took lessons from Woman during the day. They read by candlelight under the tutelage of Darling in the evenings. In fact, Darling thought of the twin-boy giants as sons. And Darcy and Digby reaped the benefits of having twice the father's love.

Then Wynter had Maestro. In the second part of every day, she strolled down the banks of the Ripplemere—stopping occasionally to dip her bare toes in the cool stream—to take her lessons on the crystal violoncello. As Wynter practiced, Maestro paced the room and held his hands together at his mouth as if in prayer. He stopped on occasion to show Wynter a new technique, turn a key to tune, or correct a misplaced hand. But as Wynter once again began to play, he resumed his march around the tiny room that overlooked the gurgling river.

In the younger days, the dissonance Wynter made when her bow struck the strings of her crystal violoncello sent Nellwyn to hide in Maestro's hood. But the din would turn to warm, evocative refrains. Nellwyn simply had to wait; it was her duty. Long hours, days, weeks, then months of afternoons wound and looped into Time's tapestry as Wynter worked in Maestro's nook by the babbling brook until cacophony became harmony. And when the melody came, on the bars and staves of Wynter's music, Nellwyn danced in the air, showering the sparkles of her delight around Maestro's homeroom.

With each initial minor success, Wind hooted his approval, but the golden leaves still clung to the trees. When Wynter mastered the positions on the neck of her instrument, a tiny chill persisted within the day's dark period when Sun departed from River's Vale. And when Wynter could play her scales by three octaves, swaying in tempo with closed eyes, the leaves rained from the trees.

LATE INTO THE NIGHT, long after Darling and Wynter had retired to their pallets for sleep, a rapping—inaudible to giants—arose outside of Darling's hut. Nellwyn awoke, stood in her self-made bed atop Wynter's headpost, and fluttered the exhaustion from her wings. She listened for the rhythm of Darling's deep snore, floated to Wynter, and lifted a white tendril from her sleeping eyes. Assured that her giant family slept soundly, she smiled as she flittered out the open window to answer her summons.

The air was still, rolling hills cast in hues of blue. Stars twinkled in the clear heights of the night. Moon slept, but on a boulder by the Ripplemere, the High Priestess illuminated the land. Formal gowns of silver and gold splayed wide on the boulder where she waited in suspended animation. Even without the help of Wind, her raven mane lifted, and she shed an azure luminescence. To the very place along the river where Wynter most enjoyed cooling her feet, Nellwyn was drawn. Priestess was smaller than an adult giant, but to Nellwyn, she outsized them all. In reality, she amounted merely to the size of Wynter at ten and one.

Priestess held out a hand; graceful, long fingers provided a platform for Nellwyn to alight and stand at eye level. Nellwyn touched her dainty feet in the palm and doubled forward in reverence. Her tiny silvery wings stretched toward the blackened sky that laid beyond Priestess's halo.

To a giant, the High Priestess would sound like a harp when she spoke. Even to Nellwyn, her words were ethereal. "My child, rise and be at ease."

Nellwyn obeyed. Priestess's palm curved, hugging her daughter. Nellwyn folded her wings, crossed her legs, and nestled into the hand of the Mother of Muses. Nellwyn sat quietly, bathed in luminosity, and wiser than to speak before spoken to. Though years had passed, her lessons were long ingrained. And as she waited, Nellwyn worried that she had somehow disobeyed what those lessons had prepared her to accomplish. Nellwyn was all too aware that Priestess watched all from The Cliffs of Change, and her messengers brought news often to where she kept her vigil.

Initial conversation was small as Priestess asked of Nellwyn how she had been in the long years. The High Priestess showered praise onto Nellwyn for being the musical inspiration to both Wynter and Maestro. Nellwyn pinkened under such a grand compliment. The Mother of Mus-es brought bright tidings from Nellwyn's kinfolk and news of kin, broth-ers and sisters, who Nellwyn had not met in her long absence. Time, the watchful mistress, held off the dawn as Priestess and Nellwyn stretched the night beyond natural bounds. Priestess listened to her child's account of the long years, and she counseled Nellwyn that her love for the giants had grown beyond duty's call.

At length, the High Priestess rose and floated above the grassy knoll, signifying their commune was coming to a close, that she'd free Time to release the night's bonds, and that Nellwyn would soon return to her Wynter. Nellwyn, faithful in servitude, flittered at her side. In what the giants would hear as a fall of hands across the harp, the High Priestess delivered the omen Nellwyn feared would one day arrive.

ON THE DAY THAT the gilt-maned giant walked into their lives, a weight settled into Nellwyn's tiny heart. The heavy beats stole the glimmer from her flutter. In counterbalance, Wynter's heart soared and climbed and flipped and flopped. Her vessel overflowed, quenching first love's thirst, every time the gilded boy giant ran up the knoll toward Darling's Hut.

"Sumor!" Wynter called and sashayed into his arms.

Amid the giants of Ripplemere, Wynter and Sumor were the only two without a dark mane. And so, they naturally found common ground in their singular duality. They were the epitome of poles—one side drawn close and the other pushed afar. While Wynter naturally faltered from heat, Sumor shuddered from cold. But when they were together, cold and hot no longer mattered. When with Sumor, Wynter could sit comfortably by a fire. And her effect on him was of equal surprise. With swimming in pools near the banks of the Ripplemere with his white-maned love, Sumor felt not the frosty bite of Wæter's fang. Together, and only together, they could relish the very things they individually found menacing.

Knowing the cycle of these things, Darling watched the pair with a torn affection. Like his forges, his heart burned warmer when Wynter could visit as he worked his metals. As such, he was pleased she'd found a companion in Sumor. But with her heart divided, he felt the loss as sharply as the blades he honed.

Nellwyn was not fond. She couldn't alight on Sumor's shoulder. He burned her toes. Nellwyn had always nestled herself closely on one of her family giants' shoulders, or she would flutter about as they went about their days.

But the season was changing, and Nellwyn was lost. When Sumor neared Darling's hut, Nellwyn sank to the front stoop. And for the first of days since Darling—carrying the bundle that was Wynter—bore her home, Nellwyn didn't follow Wynter. She stayed behind, without the will to watch her white-maned giant at Sumor's side, both unshod strolling along the Ripplemere with little fingers twined. Captiously, she told herself she would stay behind and watch over Darling.

Sumor stole many of the musical afternoons Wynter once spent with Maestro. The chill that had settled into River's Vale when Wynter's violoncello had sung lifted. Some last vermillion leaves still clung to the necks of the trees. Others blanketed their roots. Where Wynter and Sumor met, it seemed to Nellwyn that the vigilant leaves would return to green without ever sailing to the ground.

As Time balled the yarn of days and months, Nellwyn slipped from Wynter's mind. The dandelions withered, sensing that Frost had been near.

There were no seeds to chase. Nellwyn had Darling, but without her Wynter, impetus was naught.

THE NIGHT WAS UNUSUALLY warm, and inside Darling's Hut, the silence sweltered. Sumor and Wynter were out for the evening leaving only two for company. It was an odd night that Darling did not attend dinner at the other family hut, and Nellwyn worried at the stale piece of bread he chose instead. In the quiet, Darling sat by the absent fire, spent of his strength, shoulders rising and falling in uneven rhythm. Though Nellwyn perched herself on his shoulder, he hadn't the knowledge of her presence. And he was distant, lost to his wife-giant and the magical memories they'd shared before the advent of Wynter. They'd once danced and laughed and chased one another and tumbled down their grassy knoll to the flats along the Ripple-mere. And on its banks, intimacy bloomed. They'd been old to parenthood, and Candace had been at the height of radiance in her months of gestation. This night, his heart yearned for his other half.

Darling oft reflected on ages past, but on this occasion, there was cause for Nellwyn to fret. After what must have been hours enraptured by invisible flames, he drifted. Along with her sole companion, Nellwyn dozed as well. A rude jolt threw her tumbling into the air and forced to think quickly to keep from sailing to the stone floor. Darling had brutally awoken, seized by a fit of coughing.

Between rattling barks, he desperately tried to inhale through sharp hisses and wheezes. After gaining her own control, Nellwyn hovered on air waiting for Darling to breathe easily. There was naught she could do. She was helpless. When his body finally relaxed—verily slumped into the chair—she darted back to his shoulder. She whispered comforts into his ear and watched ridges on his forehead slowly relax. The weariness sinking deeper into the lines of his face painted him a prematurely old giant. Dark circles hung beneath his eyes, but the rest of his face was the white of Wynter's mane. And when the foretold shock of crimson appeared on Darling's sleeve, she knew.

With a silent word into his ear, Nellwyn encouraged Darling into bed. When he slept or even rested, she'd go for Wynter. And so, despite the warmth, she saw him safe beneath his covers. She tarried long enough to leave a silvery damp spot on the blanket, then flew through the window to find her Wynter…. To find their Wynter.

Nellwyn found Wynter with Sumor on the banks of the Ripplemere. They laughed and talked and lost themselves in one another's eyes. For a moment, but only that, Nellwyn thought maybe Darling would be alright until Wynter came home of her own accord. But his eyes set in dark caves haunted her. And she recalled the words of the Mother of Muses. This was her duty. Regardless of the cost.

She flew to Wynter's side, whispering in her ear. Then pulled her sleeve. At first, her Wynter didn't notice. She shooed her away like an annoying insect. But this was wrong, so Nellwyn persisted, flew to her shoulder, and whispered. Wynter's laugh died in mid-lilt, and her chin fell to her chest. In the corner of her eye, waiting, pleading on her shoulder, was her Nellwyn. And for the first time since Sumor came, their lifelong bond revived. Wynter raised wet, black eyes to her young love and with regret, bade him farewell. "Da . . ." She faltered as tears rolled. " . . . needs me." She stood and rushed for home.

Sumor had reached for Wynter, tried to offer his warm embrace, to console his love. But she pushed him off. When she fled, he called after, followed, but her flight was swift. He remained alone and cold. A shiver twitched up his spine, and he tucked his hands in his pockets and turned south for his own hut.

At long last Nellwyn brought her Wynter home to Darling's hut. Darling didn't stir when they arrived. Nellwyn danced by Darling's pallet, but Darling didn't notice. And for the first time in a long time, Wynter saw Nellwyn's dance. And she knew. Even before she sank to Darling's side where he lay on the pallet, tears streamed down Wynter's face—lines of frozen rivulets. Cold. He was so cold to her hands. And in another first, Wynter despised the cold. Darling had never been cold. She screamed for him to wake. She shook him to wake. She pulled at his arm, at his shoulder, at his neck. But he wouldn't open his soulful eyes.

Winter ran to get Woman and Ben. Surely, they would know what to do. They came with no question, and they had no answer. Ben shook his head. And all that Woman could do was shed her own tears and hold her near daughter close. Sobs shook Wynter's white mane and wracked the young giant's frame.

WYNTER'S FATHER WAS MUCH loved by all citizens of Ripplemere. And as funeral rites go, Darling's was a grand affair in the village of giants. The old folk had once traveled up the Ripplemere to settle in River's Vale but revered the river that ever returned to the sea. And so the legends went that the dead must be returned to the Great Sea so that their souls may cross. Men giants built Darling's boat. Women giants wove his pyre gowns. Child giants collected flowers and trinkets to travel the sea at his side. And as his nearest male giant family, Ben, Darcy, and Digby nocked the bows with arrows aflame and aimed toward the sky. The village's giants pushed the boat into the current. As it nosed toward the Great Sea, bowstrings sang, arrows arced perfectly, and the pyre blazed to life where Darling rested. And like the Ripplemere, Wynter's father returned to the Great Sea.

Though Wynter's feet remained bare, she wore her finest dress to stand with her extended giant family as her father made his final voyage. Her Sumor love stood, likewise bare of feet, dutifully by her side. On the other side, Nellwyn sat, streaming tears of glitter onto Wynter's shoulder. She cried the tears that Wynter could not cry, and Wynter felt the shimmering wet and settled into a morbid serenity.

In the days that followed, Wynter would sit in Darling's hut, numb and alone, save Nellwyn. As was her duty, Nellwyn sat with Wynter by the quiet fire as Darling did on that last frightful day. Woman brought food. Ben and Darcy and Digby checked on her regularly and ensured the hut was in order. Worry painted the family giants' faces, but Nellwyn whispered to them that Wynter would be fine. And they left, eased of their worries.

When Sumor came, he lit a fire. Wynter relished her Sumor love but couldn't shake the darkness that left with her Da. Death had stolen their giggles and shy caresses and fanciful first touches. But Sumor was there, and that alone meant more than Wynter's mourning could show.

Sumor's heat chased Nellwyn afar. She sat on the windowsill, watching, seething, and waiting for him to leave. 'Twas naught else she could do. No whispering in his ear, no suggesting he should wait. She couldn't fly that close to the flame. So she waited and checked Time's tapestry. Soon, it promised, he would go.

When Sumor departed, leaving the accursed fires, Nellwyn called upon Wind. He came and swept away the flames with a broom so fierce that the flames could not persist.

Over the weeks that followed, Sumor returned occasionally. He brought the warmth of his smile, but his golden glow seemed to fade with every visit. Wynter would walk her knoll by his side, both bare of feet and hand in his.

But she wouldn't stray afar, and he easily tired. Days greyed, and a chill hung about the mornings, and Sumor's visits spaced farther and farther apart. The hours he stayed dwindled into minutes.

Nights grew cooler, and Nellwyn whispered to Wynter day after day. In time, Wynter listened and returned to Maestro. As she began to play her crystal violoncello, the last leaves that hugged the trees released their hold and sailed to the ground. And as Wynter achieved her perfect vibrato with her violoncello, Frost crawled into River's Vale. When Wynter's pizzicato was ideally light and detached, the days grew colder still, as did the nights.

In Maestro's studio by the Ripplemere, Nellwyn whispered to both Wynter and Maestro. And Wynter achieved new heights of harmony. Soon Snow made her inaugural dance through River's Vale, turning the knolls and rocks the color of Wynter's mane.

On Sumor's last visit, a sprite rode on his shoulder. This sprite glared a flaming stare at Nellwyn as they entered Darling's hut, and Nellwyn returned the scorn with ice in her eyes. In the care of the Mother of Muses, Nellwyn had met this golden sprite and knew him by the name of Blaise. With a smile at Nellwyn, Blaise leaned in to whisper to Sumor. Loud to her ears, Nellwyn understood the message. Where she had thought ill of Blaise, she bowed her head in thanks.

Sumor held Wynter's hand, but Wynter gazed past him to the fire holding her tears at bay. He professed his love and leaked golden tears onto the floor as he told his heart their days for now were done. Sumor said that when the waters of the Ripplemere ran white and broke their shells, he would return for his Wynter love.

When Sumor and Blaise retreated from Darling's Hut down the snow-covered knoll, an icicle formed from Wynter's eye.

TIME'S NEEDLES CLICKED ON, looping threads one over the other. Age, a fearful mistress, pressed down on Ben and Woman, curved their shoulders, bent their backs, and sagged their skin. Fine lines turned into canyons across their faces. Darcy and Digby sailed down the Ripplemere to apprentice in the city by the sea. As Darling considered the giant twins near sons, he intended that they'd inherit the forges. They would assume that responsibility upon their return, and Ben would retire. Darcy and Digby, the ever-caring children giants, vowed to afford Ben and Woman peace in their twilight years. But until that time, Ben worked. And the ever-faithful friends to both Darling and Wynter, Woman and Ben, checked in each evening at Darling's hut.

Wynter helped Woman with morning chores, but in every midday and into the eves, she spent her hours with Maestro—Nellwyn never far from her side. She began to master her violoncello in new and tumultuous ways. With precision, Wynter's spiccato percussed crisply under her bow. Nellwyn fluttered around the room, sprinkling her delight's silver glitter. And a new coldness settled into the vale, felt in the bones of all the village giants upon the banks of the Ripplemere. Giants bundled when outside and huddle around inside fires. But there was ne'er a fire that burned in Darling's hut.

At the hut on the hill, Wynter and Nellwyn's connection rekindled—a bond growing and solidifying as water would freeze. And in Maestro's room by the river, they made sweet harmony. The day was short of light when Maestro said to Wynter that she had learned all he had to teach. He gifted her with the crystal violoncello and a new bow made of the most pristine silver. But this froze Wynter's heart even as Nellwyn danced and flipped and clapped within the small room by the now frozen Ripplemere. So carefully wrapped in its case, Wynter took home her treasure, leaving icy footprints in her path.

She placed the violoncello next to the rocks at the foot of her childhood home's knoll, where the ice formed in the shape of the flowing stream. Leaving Nellwyn to protect the instrument, she walked to Ben's and Woman's hut, her heart laden with her calling. This had been a long time in coming and written in the material woven by Time. It had been Nellwyn's duty when she came to the mother giant on her birthing bed. And this had been fated since Mother Giant left and Darling Giant brought home his white-maned bundle.

Wynter took her leave of Ben and Woman—icy tears on her cheeks. Before she left, she stopped by Darling's hut for one last visit. She took in the memories—where Da sat, where Da slept, where Da kissed her owies, where

Nellwyn slept, and where Sumor comforted her. Blessed though they had been, one season had passed and a new one beckoned.

In the cubby she never used that held the matches for fire she never lit, she dug. She flicked one to life, dipped the torch into the oil, touched the two, and watched it flame. She let the flames licked the curtains, then she tossed the torch on her pallet. Wynter left the hut to the flames and walked to the river. She hefted her violoncello and walked upstream with nary a look back. In her footsteps ice glazed the land behind her, and the valley fell into the deepest of winters that the settlers had ever known.

Wynter followed the Ripplemere high into the hills—but not so high as the Cliffs of Change—with Nellwyn on her shoulder. Nellwyn—her only and always companion. When Wynter tired of walking, she would stop along the Ripplemere and play on her crystal violoncello with her delicate silver bow. And where she played, ice thickened, and Snow shed flakes from the greyed skies above. Wynter walked and stopped and played and walked and stopped and played. Until she arrived at a place so vastly white and filled with peace. Nellwyn whispered to her ear, and she felt the rightness of the place. And when she played, her notes danced with Nellwyn on the air and came back to her from the rocks. They were home.

There, Wynter stayed and played as Time made on, purlwise, knitwise, slipping ever forward. Walls of ice formed around where Wynter sat. She played for long days, and walls grew higher and formed rooms. Then she played for weeks and a roof formed over her head. On and on, she played for months, and furniture formed within her new ice home. Wynter played by the river too, but always returned to her ice castle where she played all the more. In this home of ice by the frozen Ripplemere, above River's Vale yet still below the Cliffs of Change, where her Wynter landed, Nellwyn found her peace and was fulfilled. And they named their new home High Vale.

With every note that Wynter played, Nellwyn was by her side, singing encouragement into her ear and dusting their new castle silver.

WYNTER SPENT HER DAYS by the upper Ripplemere. With sun glinting from the silver bow and casting rainbows within the facets of her violoncello, Wynter closed her eyes and tilted her head toward the instrument's nape. Her hand slid up and down the fingerboard, crooning glissando. It stopped briefly on a quartertone, and only by instinct to express a rueful vibrato. As her tones and halftones and quarter tones echoed from the rock faces where they narrowed between mountains, Nellwyn sailed through the air stopping only briefly to praise or encourage her Wynter.

And as Wynter split her notes into quarters and found fresh sounds, the new spectrum heard within the vale built Wynter a throne atop the frozen Ripplemere. There she sat, giving her crystal violoncello voice. And with the new sounds warbling in the air, Wind swept down from the Cliffs of Change, adding his tune to Wynter's Anthem—swirling Wynter's mane so that strands flew long in the air. In perfect peace, Nellwyn surfed the swirling waves that Wind whisked into the air.

Snow answered the call, and her gowns whipped in Wind's sweep. In the commotion, Nellwyn oft got lost. But it was forever the clarity of Wynter's tune that marked her return to her one and only. On Wynter's Anthem, Wind led Snow in dance, carrying the tune along the Ripplemere to the village of the same name where Ben and Woman passed their days.

Time, with her ever-animated needles, wove Nellwyn's heart tighter to Wynter's using every tune of every day. And with her next stitch, she wove Wynter's heart closer to Nellwyn's, and the stars twinkled above where the violoncello sang into the nights.

IN TIME'S LONG KNITTED tapestry, the story of Wynter's Muse could be read. The story of love and passion between Darling and his giant wife could be unveiled. The story of Ben and Woman was told, and of their twin giant children, Darcy and Digby.

After long years in the city by the sea, Darcy and Digby returned to the village. They journeyed up the Ripplemere, fighting deep banks left by Snow and translucent sheets sculpted by Ice, both dancing to Wynter's song. But at last they were home to care for Ben and Woman. Then, as men giants, they brought wife giants and each of the four adult giants carried a twin baby giant. They built their own huts on the knoll where Darling's hut once stood. The female twin giant babes were Hadley and Haleigh, and they called Darcy Pa. Digby's boys were Reilly and Ridley. And they grew to young child giants as four, then to teen giants. Though the cold was bitter in their lives in River's

Vale, Ben and Woman and their progeny bonded stronger through the years as family.

But there was ever an open space for the eleventh they never discussed. It was frigid in the night when Woman spoke of her sorrow to her giant sons. She shared how she missed the daughter she never had, and her eyes stung, reddened, then overflowed into the canyons carved by Age. She bade her sons to check on their Wynter. And the good giant sons obeyed, leaving their wife giants and teen twin giants in the best of care they could imagine—Woman's. And so, bundled against Wind's sweep and Snow's flailing skirts, Darcy and Digby set out to find the source of Wynter's Anthem.

Their journey drew out, but not as long as the one from the city by the sea.

And at length they saw. The image stopped them in their labored tracks—a mane of the snowiest white tendrils floating around their small sister-like giant. She sat next to an ice palace, on an ice throne centered in the Ripplemere, and cradled an ice violoncello, and she played. She played and played, and the sun traveled from one mountain to the other as Darcy and Digby watched—somber in silence with eyes stretched.

As gloaming settled in the High Vale, Wind gathered some clouds into the sky, and their shared trance shattered. Netted snowshoes saved them from drifts that would have amounted to their waist. Those shoes hampered their speed, but they ran as best they could toward their sister-like giant. When they approached calling for Wynter over and over in animated joy, their glee reached her ears. Slowly she straightened her head and opened her charred-black eyes. Weight lifted from her stare, and she spread her pale lips into a grin Wynter thought no longer possible.

Gently, she laid down her icy instrument and silver bow, and cast away a cold blanket she didn't know she wore. True, her feet were ever bare. Never-the-less, she sailed atop the snow into her brothers' giant arms. Darcy and Digby pulled back and searched Wynter's face. While Age had drawn fine lines from the corners of their eyes and matured their brows, Wynter's was untouched by Age's pencil. Her smile was as young as the day they had left for the city, her eyes unchanged save the wisdom imparted by Time herself.

Wynter invited her near-brother giants into her icy home. Where she sat in a simple shift, they remained bundled against the cold. In this alone, Wynter frowned at their impending departure—her second loss of brothers. But they enjoyed the company for the moment, excluding Time from their conversation. Darcy spoke of Wynter's niece giants and how Hadley and Haleigh had the thickest manes in town. Digby spoke of Wynter's nephew giants—how Reilly took after Darcy and Ridley was his father's son to the last detail.

In sadder news, they also brought word of Maestro's journey o'er the frozen Ripplemere toward the Great Sea. As Wynter fought the lump in her throat, she could only speak stories of her music and her friends, Time, Wind, and Snow. While the siblings shared their tales, Nellwyn drifted from shoulder to shoulder. She'd slowed over the years, but she still left traces of silver where she'd been. Wynter knew better than to speak of Nellwyn with Darcy and Digby. As matured giants, touched by Age, they'd believe her mad to speak of the fantasies of youth.

After a too-short time, Darcy and Digby bade Wynter to return to the village by the Ripplemere and stay with Ben and Woman until their last days. But Nellwyn whispered what Wynter already knew. She would only return when the waters ran white and broke their shells, and she would return with her Sumor love. She only hoped that it would not be too late to share once again the love with Ben and Woman.

NELLWYN HAD WELCOMED DARCY and Digby. But she was also happy to see them leave without her Wynter. Nellwyn sat on her Wynter's shoulder and watched as their brother giants retreated down the Ripplemere and left High Vale for River's Vale and their huts on the knoll just outside the village. In a mirror image to Wynter's motion, Nellwyn waved from her shoulder perch.

Nellwyn's wings drooped with the loss. But Darcy and Digby had also brought news that foreshadowed change. A babe giant, white of mane, was born in the village. And the babe's mother giant had also perished in the birthing bed, leaving a single father giant and white-maned babe. The omen cut at Nellwyn's heart, but only brought hope to Wynter's.

In the time that followed, Wynter's music faltered. She would catch her mistakes and in frustration, leave her instrument propped on the ice throne for hours on end. Nellwyn fretted over this, wringing her hands and pacing her mistress's shoulder ledge. In the hours where Wynter left her music to wander High Vale, Snow would no longer dance or flare her skirts near the ice castle, Wind lost his vigorous sweep, and Nellwyn grew weak.

The High Priestess had taught Nellwyn about the cycle of seasons and understood that Time's tapestry was writing yet another change. But even so, she tucked her wings and stayed close to Wynter, holding out the remnants of hope.

In the stitches of Time, Wynter's musical duties waned. The hours that her violoncello sat by her throne grew into days that the instrument rested in the worn wooden case inside the ice castle. And Time pulled the yarn of the days into weeks, then months. One day on Wynter's stroll, a sharp crack awoke Nellwyn from one of her—as of late, more frequent—naps. Wynter padded toward the sound and found a split in the ice of the Ripplemere, running long beside her throne. Nellwyn whispered to her Wynter that the time was near.

More days passed, and Wynter lost her vibrato, her pizzicato, and her glissando. Even so, her heart felt lightened of the burden. And Nellwyn slept more and more in the crevice at Wynter's collar.

IT WAS A WARM and moonless night in High Vale, and Wynter slept. Nellwyn heard the beckon of rapping outside the ice castle, checked on her Wynter, and glided out to meet the High Priestess. She had summoned her before, and this time, Nellwyn better understood the calling.

As with the last time, Nellwyn sailed to High Priestess's hugging hand and came to rest with crossed legs and folded wings. The azure luminosity in the night around Mother of Muses spoke a different message this time. The light beckoned Nellwyn to come home. Nellwyn had known that Time would purl this stitch, but that didn't hold back the dull glitter of her tears that pooled into High Priestess's hand.

Unlike the time before when the Mother of Muses had visited, there was no talk of how Nellwyn's work progressed. And as was always the case, High Priestess's celestial message came to Nellwyn. "The waters will run white tomorrow, and their shells will break. Say your goodbyes, and return unto me, sweet daughter. It is time for you to rest until your next duty calls."

Before Nellwyn left with the Mother of Muses, she flew slowly back into the castle where Wynter slept. As she spiraled High Vale, a silent, last, and lonely flight, she noticed the sharp edges of Wynter's palace had curved as if they wept for this moment. Nellwyn soared to Wynter and planted glittering kisses on her forehead, her cheeks, her ears, her chin, and lastly, the lids of her eyes near her dark lashes. With a final glistening tear that landed on Wynter's shoulder, Nellwyn returned to High Priestess.

MORN ARRIVED, AND WYNTER awoke. Sun warmed her castle as never before. In the warmth, there was also a void. Wynter searched the castle. Ran from room to room. Looked high, low, in every corner. Sank to the floor. There was no sign of her Nellwyn, her life's companion, the spirit who'd always been at her side. A frozen tear melted on her cheek, and her shift absorbed the water of the thawing floor.

She lifted her head and listened. Outside, the Ripplemere babbled through High Vale. Her love had said that when the waters of the Ripplemere ran white and broke their shells, he would return for his Wynter love. With no sign of her silvery sprite, but a hope she dared not foster, she rose and tiptoed out of doors.

And as he had promised, Sumor stood on the bank in front of white waters rushing down the valley, free of their iced shells, and toward River's

Vale. Browned grasses peeked through what snow remained, and Wynter rushed across the snow dappled lawn into Sumor's arms. As he thawed her heart, the tears streamed down her face and dripped from her chin. And she tucked Nellwyn into a corner of her heart—ne'er to be removed.

As the love once known by Sumor and Wynter rekindled, an empyreal voice flooded High Vale. "Enjoy one another … But Wynter, you have a final charge. Return to River's Vale to instruct the white-maned babe. Take up residence in Maestro's cottage by the babbling brook. And wait for your sign."

In the harp notes that trailed and long silence that followed, Sumor and Wynter did as High Priestess bade and thoroughly enjoyed one another before they started the journey down to River's Vale. Snow afforded the couple their privacy, but Wind whistled his approval through High Vale.

THE LAND TURNED GREEN when Sumor and Wynter strolled into the village. The first huts that Wynter saw were on the knoll where she once lived with Darling. They were quiet. She and Sumor both smiled and cuddled closer together as they walked by the knoll and found the home of Ben and Woman. Here, the entire family gathered. Woman had become a tiny bent giant with wisps of grey tendrils falling from her bun. Ben had likewise stooped, but the fires of the forges still danced in his eyes. Darcy and Digby looked more like Wynter remembered Ben, and it warmed her heart even more. They introduced Hadley and Haleigh and the boys, Reilly and Ridley. Sumor and Wynter were the only two adult giants who Age had not touched, but the village accepted their youth. And Woman and Ben named them family.

Sumor and Wynter made their home in the cottage near the Ripplemere. Maestro's instruments and studio was just as Wynter recalled. She dusted the grime from the counter, the chairs, and the music stand. Wynter shed a single tear as she went about the work of tidying. It glistened as Nellwyn's had when it hit the counter.

Through it all, Time continued her knitting. She looped days into weeks and purled weeks into months. And all the while, Wynter and Sumor loved one another. Wynter no longer feared the heat. Days grew warmer and longer until one bright and hot day on the banks of the Ripplemere. Sumor held Wynter's hand. They soaked their feet in the water.

With golden pools in his eyes and cracking voice, Sumor whispered, "My darling, Wynter… You had your time of duty, but now it is mine. I must travel to High Vale as you once did. We shall only see each other again once we cross the Great Sea."

As they sat on the bank with grass growing beneath, their brows pressed together, falling tears swirled together on their hands. And in those tears, an image formed—High Priestess in her formal robes on the Cliffs of Change watching over their time to part.

IN TIME'S TAPESTRY THAT followed through the hot years, Wynter spent time alone in her cottage or with her extended family of giants. She watched Darcy and Digby grow with their wives, their twins take the trip down the Ripplemere to the city by the sea for school, and they all celebrated the lives of Ben and Woman as they went together on their final voyage across the great sea.

Age caught up with Wynter faster than it had with her near-brothers, and she came once again to appear the same in age as Darcy and Digby. And at long last, a dark-maned giant—still untouched by Age—brought a young white-maned giant into Wynter's studio. Through stiff joints and tight muscles, Wynter knelt beside the white-maned boy giant and asked, "What's your name, young lad?"

With shy charred eyes, he looked to his dad, then back and answered, "My name is Wynter."

"And dear boy, your friend who sits on your shoulder, what is his name?"

His eyes grew wide. "Nevyn," he whispered.

She swallowed the well behind her eyes, smiled, and said to the boy giant, "You may call me Maestra."

Continue reading for the first chapter of my upcoming series:

The Serpentine Throne

CALL OF THE STORM SORCERER

THE SERPENTINE THRONE BOOK 1

A PREVIEW CHAPTER

BY

SUSAN STRADIOTTO

PART ONE

Ascension

The Fifth Age

Princess Mairynne Evangale

ONE

Nantai in Mourning

Generations have passed since the Ryū Wars, the age when the great dragons and people split and became mortal foes. Yet the Nantai people, my people, remain. I have never met one of the Ryū, the dragons of old. Nor have I felt the ties of companionship, but our people's lessons were ingrained. Both represented the purest variety of evil. From before I gained knowledge of letters, my sisters and I clung to stories Father had told. Karynne, Shanynne, and I had gathered at his feet near the throne crafted from the last dragon's skin and bone and scale, and we listened to Tennō Atheryn read from Stormskeep's annals. His voice had resonated in my blood as he'd painted the history of companionship, the most toxic of bonds between a dragon and a person.

The stories had been as exciting as they were dangerous. During the time at my father's heel, I'd been too young to understand or wield my storm sorcery with any bit of control, but my sisters would stir small gusts of wind, animating dyed sands to enact the scenes. Between Father's booming narration and the miniature scenes, I'd giggle and clap and thoroughly enjoy the show.

Over the course of the histories read, it became clear that the ryūbond drove people to commit acts unimaginable. Father wouldn't read to us of the treachery, but he did share one story—a story that kept me awake in dark hours for many moons, the story of the people's first emperor: Tennō Makenyn, the Scarred. After surviving the ritual that peeled away the soul-deep bond between him and the blackest dragon, a Kuroidragon, he wore the scars for the remainder of his days and walked hunchbacked, limping as he went.

I closed and reopened my eyes slowly, returning to my chambers, to the now, and to myself, my shoulders laden under the weight of both the memory and the mourning robes my attendants draped about my shoulders. The material well-positioned, Mother Feathergale scurried to the adjacent room to retrieve the lengths of fabric that would secure the garments and further restrict any ability to breathe easily. Desperate to put away the heavy garments proscribed for the sixty days and nights of mourning my father had declared in the wake of my mother's death, I asked, "How many more?" I'd asked the same question every morn as they attended to my attire.

Yet my friend and attendant answered readily, "A dozen days remain, Lady Mairynne." Jessa bobbed in deference to my impending position.

I clasped her shoulders and waited for her gaze to lift, to meet mine, then said, "Please don't treat me so. I'm the same person I was ten days ago before Tennō Atheryn Evangale went missing, and I'll be the same person tomorrow and after this period of mourning has passed."

"Yes, Lady Mairy—"

I squeezed to silence her formal objection. Looking sternly into her worried eyes, I said, "Simply Mairynne. The same Mairynne who has been at your side since we were younglings." When her tension eased, mine did the same. I gulped air, rolling my shoulders back to support the robes' weight.

Employed by my parents to care for their royal children and known to us as Mother Feathergale, Jessa's blooded mother returned to my chambers. She looked small in comparison to the swaths of belting material overflowing her grasp, but it didn't appear a burden. She used her sorcery, stirred a minor wind to carry the heavy belts, and she simply guided them toward the bed. I released my dear friend and turned to face the mirror. The royal mourning garments were extensive, so Jessa went to help. As they returned, I lifted my arms to receive the finishing touches.

To my attendants and to the holy Triad should they be listening, I raised my chin and voice. "How are the city's people handling the loss? And the people beyond?"

Mother Feathergale revolved around me, binding my body with the blessed robes so I might feel embraced by my loved one lost. She worked proficiently and spoke with a cutting absence when she answered, "They await patiently, per tradition. And you shouldn't toil over the matter now. The Triad intends for you to focus on healing during the quiet time. Decreed by the blessed emperor and respected by all castes and the casteless alike."

In the long days while I waited idly, and more so within that moment, I felt inclined to curse the traditions, shun the robes, and escape the stony walls that bound me to the castle and citadel alone. I longed for action, to discover if others believed—as did I—that Father still lived. I yearned to see how the people reacted to the loss of both their rulers. Still working to gain necessary confidence in my convictions, I spoke more quietly, with uncertainty, and voiced words that I dared not speak to anyone less trusted than Jessa and Mother Feathergale, "With all that has happened, do you not believe the rituals selfish at all?"

Mother Feathergale finished securing the ends of the obi and came to face me, her eyes blinking then widening with bewilderment. "Why ever would it be selfish, Mairynne?"

Lowering my eyes, I smiled ruefully. Had I truly expected her to hold beliefs outside of those handed down for generations?

My aging attendant wiped her palms on her apron and opened her arms to me with a smile. I fell willingly inside as she offered me what comfort she could, but in the end, she pushed me away with a solemn look, misty eyes, and slight nod. "There, you're ready for the day. Your mother would be proud. Your father too," she added.

I swallowed against the sudden burn in my throat. Her gaze left mine as she inspected the belts, making tiny adjustments while I, too, gathered myself. I would not cry. I'd done enough of that since my mother's death. For my father to have disappeared so soon after, I felt cracked, as if a fissure ran through my soul. The realm seemed to feel the same, and the recovery of a people having lost their leaders lurked in the wings as everyone respected one of our most sacred beliefs and waited for the rites of mourning to pass. While I loathed the clothing and sense of confinement, I also dreaded the completion of the sixty days and nights and the duty that awaited once mourning passed.

I picked up my skirts and lumbered toward the door.

"Mairynne," Mother Feathergale called, "we still need to bind your hair."

Pushing my chin higher, I said, "I think I'll leave it loose."

"But—"

I held a hand forward to halt the propriety. I would wear the clothing, but I refused the hair. Finishing my day with a headache from constant pull was the last of my desires. Traditionally, the decision may have been blasphemous, but there were no formal ceremonies this day. Outside of going to the Citadel, I wouldn't meet any of my people. My sisters and the Triad's priests could tolerate my small defiance.

The older woman clasped her hands and put on a smile. "You have always been a headstrong child. Your mother and I have always been there to encourage your determination." She curtsied. "As you will."

To my friend, I asked, "Jessa, will you walk with me?"

She lifted her own robes of mourning, although significantly less encumbering than mine, and joined me at the door. I envied her lack of station, but I'd little choice to my own. These walls held me as did the propriety and custom. The robes simply ensured I couldn't breathe.

Before leaving, I turned. "Thank you, Mother Feathergale. For everything."

Despite my sense of suffocation, I'd been fortunate to have gained my majority having two motherly figures in my life, my best friend's mother and the woman who had borne my sisters and me into the world. Before her death, Noralynne Evangale had possessed strength and compassion revered by all castes of our people. Nantai's casteless and Small Folk had also loved the empress, a fondness rulers before her couldn't claim. As I turned down the hall toward the bridge, I grasped at the two small tokens that hung on a chain around my neck; one stone felt constantly warm against my skin and the other constantly cold. The soldiers who found Mother had pulled the cold thing from her hand after recovering her twisted body from the borders of the

Evernight Marshes near the Great Sands. The warm stone, I had found on my father's pillow the morning he, Tennō Atheryn Evangale, had disappeared.

WITHIN NANTAI'S JEWEL CITY of Arashi, Stormskeep Castle hugged the side of a cliff high above a great waterfall. We exited the castle proper onto a wide landing then moved toward the bridge crossing high above Sundai Falls. Our steps carried us onward over the narrow bridge to the citadel beyond where my sisters and I would meet with priests and receive updates on the upcoming rites. Though I'd grown up in the people's central city, I had no memories at Stormskeep in which the sound of water flowing over stone did not provide ambiance. Even in the most remote corners of the castle, if I were to listen, I could have heard the wooshing and splashes. Now, as we crossed the bridge over the falls slowly, the ever-present sound soothed my nerves.

Each tentative foot forward caused the bridge to sway, and I questioned my balance. Should I fall, I could call the wind to carry me to safety, but it would incite commotion and angst over my wellbeing amongst any people gathered below in the daylight hours. Today, I wished for privacy, and the need to face my sisters as well as the Triad was burden enough, so I took care and held the rough rope railing as I walked shoulder-to-shoulder with Jessa. She, on the other hand, moved freely in her light-weight robes.

Again, I envied her.

"You seem distant today," Jessa said, turning to face me then quickly back to our path.

I breathed deeply and sighed. "My mind is clouded with what's needed to complete the rituals. Day forty-eight, you said?"

"Mmmm, yes."

"We only have three rites remaining, and then we can dispense with the sadness that hangs over our people."

"Over your people, Lady Mairynne. Afterward, do you intend to prepare for ascension?"

I stopped both walking and breathing, but my question spilled out anyway. "Why would you ask such a question so carelessly?" I said, scanning for onlookers.

She fumbled to find decorum and the right response. "My apologies, Lady. I just figured we were alone and that the sounds of the falls would mask the question."

I had wounded her. For her to have asked only reflected my own worry; I had scolded where I should not have. "No, Jessa, it is I who should apologize. My ascension is the expectation of the people, is it not?" Truly, this was no answer, but I hoped it was enough to appease her curiosity.

It sufficed. She eased, looped an arm through mine, and offered her strength to supplement my own.

Half-way across the bridge, I stopped and turned to face the falls. Mist wafted up on the wind from the rocks, cooling my face and stirring my loose hair. To my oldest friend, I said, "If—and that is a big if—I do, I've much to prepare over the next twelve days. I'm not ready to be empress, and I fear I am not truly ready for the burden."

"Mairynne, there is reason—"

"I know the reason behind all of this." Shaking my head, I grasped her hand eased my words for her benefit. "Along with my sisters, my parents groomed me for this very thing, but the time came far sooner than I thought." I paused, looking down at our clasped hands. "They…my parents, that is, were taken from us before their time."

Jessa hugged me around the shoulders, her simple touch, silence, and acceptance offering more strength than she knew.

"Anyway," I said at last and a mite ruefully, "my remaining family awaits my arrival. We'd best be on our way."

Inside the citadel, we turned to the right and made for the Triad's meeting chambers behind the temple proper. At a long table, the Triad's clergy sat in chairs in a seemingly random pattern, each reading from a scroll. My sisters and their first advisers also awaited. Karynne sat at the table's head, and I wondered how early she'd arrived to secure the seat of power. To her left, Yasmynne leaned close to her consort, Nestryn.

Upon my father's disappearance, my sisters had wasted no time in choosing and announcing their first advisers. The thought caused my stomach to churn. Nestryn had now elevated to Yasmynne's first adviser, yet they sat too close, too intimately for an official proceeding. Their manner had always been an open display of affection, and they paid little heed to the company present. Poised behind Karynne, the powerful, more seductive Imrythel Sandsgale rested one hand on the back of my sister's chair. She, Karynne's chosen, was almost too much to behold, ebony hair flowing, one eye covered with a black veil while the other peered back, an uncommonly piercing green. Merely looking upon her, I felt out of place in my own skin and fought the urge to fidget.

Wearing attire that mirrored my own, Karynne stood and closed the distance between us. Having our father's height, she looked down, grasped my shoulders, and folded me into a hug. "Mairynne," she said. "How are you doing this morning?"

"I do wish we didn't have to do this today," I answered. "But if we must, let us begin."

Karynne's glance flickered past me to Jessa but returned quickly, and with a smile, she nudged me toward the chair at her right. "Sister, why is your hair unbound?"

Yasmynne surfaced from her whispers and flipped a hand in their oldest sister's direction. "Oh Kahry, let her be. This is our only obligation today."

Across the table, I gave Yasmynne a thankful, but questioning stare.

The elderly priest cleared his throat and rolled his scroll. "With you all here, we are ready to proceed."

The other clergy, each a Hallowgale by tradition of those raised to serve the Triad, followed his lead in stowing their reading.

The much younger priestess said, "Edamyn, we should excuse the advisers." The notes in Tasmynne's voice rang high and clear as she looked meaningfully from Nestryn to Imrythel then to my friend Jessa.

Though I had not announced a first adviser of my own, all assumed that I'd chosen my dearest friend. I had not, as I refused to accept that my father and our emperor wouldn't return. Jessa accepted her dismissal, but the others looked to my sisters awaiting permission. Imrythel was the last to leave and made a show of pulling closed the heavy double doors.

Once alone with our holy counsel, the senior Hallowgale, Edamyn began with the traditional opening blessing of the Triad. "May Atun, the All Seer, guide us today."

The others, Arlyn and Tasmynne dipped their heads acknowledging the tradition.

Arlyn offered the second invocation. "May Otarr, the Sun Seer alight our way."

"And may the Moon Seer, Selene, give us wisdom," Tasmynne finished.

"Arlyn, do you wish to begin?" Edamyn held a shaky hand in the direction of Otarr's high priest.

"Yes, thank you." He sat straighter in his chair, folding his hands atop the table. "Otarr has shown Kōgō Noralynne Evangale the way to her next life. Time has passed enough that we may sweep the mandala sands. Emissaries from the Fire Forgers have delivered the phials. We have sorcerers at the ready to hold off any storms so we may ensure Otarr may gaze upon us. We are ready for the eighth and ninth rites to begin three days hence."

I stifled the urge to groan at the thought of two long, sweltering days under the sun overseeing the sweeping of the sands, and there would be no reprieve on the third as we handed out the phials of the ritual sands to the people. My sisters and I listened with aplomb as was our duty. Discussion continued between the Hallowgales around positioning and other technical aspects required for the ceremony, and I exchanged looks with my sisters from time to time until the insignificant details had run their course.

Tasmynne moved on. "As to the final rite, the caretakers are tending to the nymphs around the clock, keeping their ecosystem within the precise condition to encourage the final transformation. The nymphs are preparing for their final molting cycle and are on schedule to emerge from the water and shed their skin just in time for the Rite of Release." Tasmynne relaxed back in her chair as she finished, clearly satisfied with her preparation in the Nantai Rituals of Mourning.

In the swift pause that followed, Karynne leaned forward, resting her elbows on the table. "Very well," she said. "It seems all is on track to complete honoring our mother."

Just as swiftly, she turned on me and pinned me with a sharp gaze. Instinctively, I tensed, feeling my fingers digging into the wooden arm of the chair. As I scanned the others in the room, every person's focus also rested on me.

She continued, "Mairynne, are you prepared to tend to your duties once the rites are complete?"

I swallowed though my mouth felt suddenly dry. I'd foreseen this question, but that didn't make answering easier. Ultimately, I wasn't intent on abdication, only avoidance. "If you inquire about my understanding, I'm versed in the expectation that we begin preparation for my ascension."

"Expectation be damned to the hells," said Karynne. "What I wonder is if you actually plan to begin the proceedings. It is clearly what Father wanted; him having written his directive into the Stormskeep annals that you, his third daughter, shall be his successor to the throne of Stormskeep."

My shoulders tightened, my neck pinched, so I rolled my head to relieve the strain and sighed. While I adored my eldest sister, she could temper her rash demeanor with a smattering of tact. Leveling my voice as much as possible, I replied, "We have twelve sacred days remaining before I must face this decision, Kahry. Can we tend to our grief for now?"

Yasmynne reached across the table to offer me a hand. I accepted and awaited her thoughts. Her gaze flitted to our older sister, then with a gentle smile, she said, "Of course we will respect the rituals, but you should know that our people are becoming lost without a leader. Our advisers say there have been some disturbances in the streets, and we've heard rumors from the other castes."

The matter of unrest within the people concerned me more than my place on the throne; however, I needed time. "Twelve days," I responded, rigid and unmoving as I stated my will, "Only then will I address the topic of inheritance."

"You must at least name your first adviser officially and make the decree in the annals," Karynne continued, seemingly searching for a way to force me to address my impending duty. "Jessa, though she is dear to you, is not an appropriate royal adviser."

To her, I pressed my lips into a tight line. There was little clarity in my mind as to why she believed Imrythel or Nestryn met the so-called requirements, but now wasn't the time to discuss. Pressing that issue would have only ensnared me in further conversation about a topic I wasn't ready to address. I turned to the elderly priest at my right and asked, "Is there aught to discuss regarding the rites?"

Edamyn Hallowgale replied, "No, Lady Mairynne, we have concluded our business."

I stood; the chair whined against the floor as my momentum pushed it backward. My sisters both followed my cue. I hugged Karynne formally, then Yasmynne, who grabbed onto me and squeezed tight, showing the affection she wore in her very bones. As I broke the hug, I stated again, "Twelve days. It's not long. I value our sisterhood beyond what you will ever know, but this acceptance is mine and mine alone. I must come to it in my own time. Once I have decided, you both will be the first to know." On those words, I made for the doors.

Hot moisture gathered about my belts as I pulled one door inward enough to squeeze through and make my escape. In the foyer, I turned toward the open-air sanctuary overlooking Stormkeep Falls, desperate for some relief. In my path, Imrythel stood. My level gaze rested at the hollow in her long, graceful throat. Clenching my teeth, I lifted my chin to make eye contact.

IMRYTHEL RAISED A HAND and softly ran a long finger down my face, the trail she traced burning a line from near my eye, down, and along my jawline. Against the urge to flinch away, I held myself in place and waited.

"Your sister cares deeply for you, for the Evangale legacy, and for the Nantai people," she said, her voice deeper and more seductive than a woman's voice had a right to be. "I see many questions written on your face."

Unclear what she suggested, I reminded myself that Tennō Atheryn's decree named me successor and trained my features into a mask of solemnity. Versed in the ways of Nantai politics, the woman before me carried a manner about her that embodied power and temptation. She used her height to exude an air of authority while her curves dripped with sensuality and the veil she wore covering one eye cast an air of mystery about her. In choosing her first adviser, my sister Karynne clearly sought to use these skills to her advantage. As Father had instructed us all, I measured my words. "Thank you, Imrythel. In these days, I take comfort in my sisters as we, along with the rest of the Nantai people, pay due respect to my mother's memory."

"Yes." She clasped her hands behind her back, and her gaze dropped for only a moment before she continued, "Well, do remember that you must have trust in those who love you."

I donned an appeasing smile and gave credit to the truth in her words. "Well put. Now, if you'll excuse me, I'd like some time in sanctuary with my thoughts."

As I moved around her, Jessa stepped to my side.

"Lady Mairynne," Imrythel called.

I turned to see that Karynne had joined her.

Regally, they stood shoulder-to-shoulder as Imrythel added, "Karynne and I both are to champion your path to the throne; your advocates if you will." She tipped her head forward in a move so small it almost escaped me.

Yet now was no time to bend in my conviction. Giving a single nod, I passed through the grand archway leaving them to their will and my dear friend in my wake. Inside, I clasped both of Jessa's hands and asked her to wait without as well. I wished nothing more than to be alone with my thoughts and prayers to Atun and his children, Otarr and Selene.

For time I didn't count, I knelt at Selene's altar and called a wind to bring mist from the falls and cool me as I contemplated. At intervals, I spoke aloud to the gods, seeking guidance. I received no answer to the questions in my mind. Atun didn't tell me why someone slayed my mother; Otarr wouldn't grant me the knowledge of where my father had gone; and Selene gave me no guidance regarding my unsettling feeling that Tennō Atheryn still lived. Fighting a burning behind my eyes, I lifted my face to the skies and cried, "Father, what would you do in my place?"

An unseen, but rich and familiar voice answered, "I know not what Tennō Atheryn would do."

"Thalaj," I breathed, wiping a tear that'd strayed down my cheek. I stood and moved in his direction.

He stepped from the shadows, from one of the apses set into the outer wall. Exempt from wearing full robes of mourning, Stormskeep guards dressed in light leathers with a red sash from shoulder to hip, easily removed should the need arise. Weapons remained accessible.

"Your robes flatter, but I do prefer your hair unbound," Thalaj said as he approached.

"These robes are better suited to my sisters than they are to me." I moved in his direction, but before I reached him, he dropped his eyes and turned slightly away. The movement prevented the embrace I'd intended, and my shoulders felt heavy again, this time not from the robes. "Will you not give me the comfort of holding me?"

"Lady Mairynne, you know it's blasphemous." He ran a hand over his braids to the throng at the base of his skull.

Flinching at the formality, I snapped, "We have done nothing blasphemous."

"If anyone sees us within in an embrace, my head would decorate the spikes at the Stormskeep gates."

"No one can persecute you for offering comfort in this time." I searched his face.

He warned me off with a look and said, "That my mother is a Storm Sorcerer is insignificant here. That she chose a Frost Fighter as my father makes me unworthy. There is the matter of contamination that is punishable only by death."

"Thalaj," I huffed. "You know that I do not hold with the caste beliefs. And you know that my mother and father supported my stance."

"And how has that worked for them?" He challenged while rubbing a gloved thumb over the hilt of his scimityne. Seconds later, he realized the splinter his words pushed under my skin. "I'm sorry." He dropped his head and silently moved to the railing beyond the alters, leaning over toward the falls.

I joined him. As he turned to face me, I could feel his eyes, and unable to handle the silence, I pressed, "Why must such things come between people drawn to one another?" My words were more of a complaint than a question.

He answered anyway, "Mairynne, you know how to change this."

I turned to him abruptly, and questioned, "Not you too?" Everyone pressed for my ascension, but I'd hoped the man who'd become a fixture in my life, as our protector, wouldn't join causes with the masses.

Thalaj looked down. "It is not my place to counsel you, but royal decrees are our only mechanism for change amidst our people. An emperor or empress must formally write them into the annals under the Hallowgales' supervision. I see little other course of action."

Though his motivations were different, he'd joined in the opinion of the majority and clearly wished for my ascension. As such, I considered the personal conversation over, nodded, and switched to business. "Have you any word of my father from your network?"

"I do not."

"And you believe he will not return?"

"That, I cannot say for certain. Though there has never been a period when Tennō Atheryn has been absent from his castle for so many unexcused days."

I reached out over the railing toward the rushing water, calling for the mist. I concentrated allowing the power to pool in my heart and pulled with my sorcery. A small storm gathered in my hands. Watching the mist turn into tiny thunderheads and feeling rain begin to fall onto my palms, I absently asked, "Then why do I have this overwhelming sensation that he lives?"

Thalaj sighed. "I don't know, Lady Mairynne."

Silence except for rushing water and tiny sounds of thunder cocooned us on the balcony. Calling on my magic offered a much-needed distraction and allowed an idea to bloom in the back of my mind. Stormskeep annals. The histories of our people written by rulers through the ages would surely offer guidance. I clapped my hands together, extinguishing the storm, and said, "I think . . ."

"What?" He searched my face. "What do you think?"

I glanced at him with a quirked brow and grin. "You, and everyone else, will see." Turning to the arched entry, I called the wind for assistance with my burdening robes and walked lightly and swiftly toward the foyer. Behind me, Thalaj's heels clicked upon the marble as he followed.

My sisters, their advisers, and the clergy still loitered in the foyer, likely awaiting my return. Jessa rushed toward me when I emerged; Karynne, Imrythel, and the clergy turned, but Yasmynne and Nestryn continued in their whispered conversation. I lowered my eyes, feeling a stab of jealousy over their happiness, but I refocused quickly. "Jessa," I said. "Send word to each member of Tennō Atheryn's advisory council that we will meet first thing on the morrow within the royal court."

"Of course, Lady Mairynne." Jessa curtsied, then scurried to the bridge and onward to complete the chore I'd demanded.

Yasmynne turned, alerted by my command. Karynne took a breath to speak.

Before she could utter words, I held up both hands to forestall her and said, "My sisters, Hallowgales of the Triad, Imrythel and Nestryn as first advisers, you will all be in attendance as well at the ninth bell."

Karynne asked, "What is the meaning of the meeting?"

"You will learn with the others. Yasmynne, can you ensure that Aunt Nadialynne receives word and is present as well?"

She nodded, seeming uncertain and startled by the sudden demands which worked well for my taste.

My intent could remain a mystery for the time. I turned to Thalaj before anyone else could utter more questions. I thought to ask for his company, but reconsidered and demanded, "You will escort me to the royal library."

ABOUT THE AUTHOR

SUSAN STRADIOTTO WRITES FANTASY for New Adult and later Young Adult audiences, with story lines that are enjoyable for adults too. Themes frequently focus on relationship situations, family situations, coming of age, and finding oneself or one's destiny. But from time to time, she'll write something for worldbuilding purposes like the folktale *The Wanderer and the Devil*.

Susan also enjoys reading and reviewing other fantasy books and blogs about worldbuilding topics on her website https://www.susanstradiotto.com. She enjoys spending game-days with her family. They often play Dungeons & Dragons or a handful of other strategic and worldbuilding games. She lives in Eden Prairie with a wonderful husband, two of her three adult children, and two fur-children.

STAY TUNED!

THE SERPENTINE THRONE SERIES WILL CONTINUE ON MARCH 30, 2021

This begins a five-book series. The COMPLETE series will release throughout the spring and summer over five months beginning with *Call of the Storm Sorccerer* on March 30.

IN THE MEANTIME...

CONNECT WITH ME ON SOCIAL FOR ONGOING UPDATES

Note: my newsletter subscribers will get the first insights and best of the best in goodies, but I'll also be sharing lots of fun stuff and giveaways on social in advance of the launches. Instagram and Goodreads are my faves.

Instagram:
@susanstradiotto
or https://www.instagram.com/susanstradiotto/

Goodreads:
https://www.goodreads.com/susanstradiotto
Go ahead and **friend me** instead of just following! I love to see what my readers are reading and reviewing!

Facebook page:
https://www.facebook.com/susanstradiottoauthor

Twitter:
@StradiottoS
or https://twitter.com/StradiottoS

Pinterest:
https://www.pinterest.com/sstradiotto/